For Steven, Susan, and Fiona
—L. G.

For Tomás
—J. S.

SIMON & SCHUSTER BOOKS FOR YOUNG READERS

An imprint of Simon & Schuster Children's Publishing Division

1230 Avenue of the Americas, New York, New York 10020

Text copyright © 2018 by Louise Greig

Illustrations copyright © 2018 by Júlia Sardà

Originally published in Great Britain in 2018 by Egmont UK Limited.

First US edition 2019

SIMON & SCHUSTER BOOKS FOR YOUNG READERS is a trademark of Simon & Schuster, Inc.

For information about special discounts for bulk purchases, please contact

Simon & Schuster Special Sales at 1-866-506-1949 or business@simonandschuster.com.

The Simon & Schuster Speakers Bureau can bring authors to your live event. For more information or to book an event,

contact the Simon & Schuster Speakers Bureau at 1-866-248-3049 or visit our website at www.simonspeakers.com.

The text for this book was set in Walbaum MT.

The illustrations for this book were rendered digitally.

Manufactured in China

0719 SCP

2 4 6 8 10 9 7 5 3 1

CIP data for this book is available from the Library of Congress.

ISBN 978-1-5344-3908-5

ISBN 978-1-5344-3910-8 (eBook)

Sweep

By Louise Greig

Illustrated by Júlia Sardà

Simon & Schuster Books for Young Readers

New York London Toronto Sydney New Delhi

Ed in a good mood is a very nice Ed.

Ed in a bad mood is not.

And Ed was in a bad mood.

Not one of those tiny whirlwinds in a teacup
that blow over before they have even begun.

No, this mood swept over him in a raging storm and stuck.

It began as something small . . .

really small, hardly a thing at all.

But before Ed knew it, the something had grown, gathered pace, and swept him off down a path.

Ed's bad mood thought this was a wonderful idea.

But the things that got in Ed's way did not.

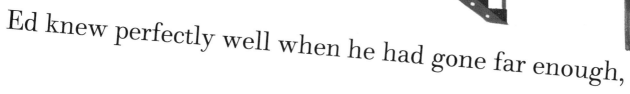

Ed knew perfectly well when he had gone far enough,

but he could not bring himself to say, "Okay, that will do."

So, on he stormed a bit farther. And a bit farther still.

Until, suddenly the whole thing became **bigger** than him!

Of course, if Ed had looked up he would
have noticed the beautiful things,
the things that always made his heart sing.

But he refused to lift his eyes.
The ground was a lot more interesting,
or so his bad mood told him.

Everything seemed against him.

But that just made him even more determined.

He dug in his heels and kept going.

Just Ed and his **bad mood.**

*Is this **really** worth it?* he asked himself.

Yes, his bad mood decided, though Ed did wonder a little.

Now his bad mood had swept through the whole town.
The birds had stopped singing.
The flowers had disappeared.

This whole thing was affecting everyone and everything.

Good, thought Ed's bad mood,
but really Ed was beginning to wish it had
all blown over like a whirlwind in a teacup.

Everything grew dark and Ed was getting tired and hungry.
He was finding it harder and harder to keep this up.

Surely he could not give up now?
Not when he had gone to all this trouble.
That would be crazy.

But **something** had to change.

And then something did change.

A new wind whipped up.

It began as something small,

really small,

that became bigger,

bigger
than Ed.

Suddenly everything looked different.
The world looked **brighter**.

For a moment Ed felt rather silly.
Had he **really** gone to all that effort for nothing?

But at least it had
cleared the air.

It had even blown something his way.

Something that made him look up.

It lifted his mood.
Higher and higher—up to the sky.

And suddenly he noticed beauty all around him.

It swept him away.

As for his bad mood, it vanished into thin air.

Now, when it looks as if Ed might,
just **might**, spiral into a bad mood
and sweep down **that path** again,

he thinks twice.

His first thought is *Will I?*

and his second thought is . . .

Or not?